Penguin Days

by SARA LEACH

Illustrations by Rebecca Bender

pajamapress

For Duane—S.L.

For my mom—R.B.

PRAISE FOR *Slug Days*

by SARA LEACH

Illustrations by Rebecca Bender

Honors

2019 Chocolate Lily Award: Chapter Book/
Early Novel nominee

2017 Foreword INDIES: Juvenile Fiction
Award finalist

2018 ALA Schneider Family Book Award finalist

2018 *Horn Book*, "August 2018 Back-to-School Horn
Book Herald: Intermediate" selection

2018 *Huffpost* "17 Children's Books That Promote
Understanding of Autism" selection

2018 *A Mighty Girl* "A Different Way of Thinking:
20 Books About Autistic Mighty Girls" selection

2018 USBBY Outstanding International Books List –
Grades 3-6 selection

2018 CCBC *Best Books for Kids & Teens*
Starred Selection

Reviews

"*Slug Days* wisely presents autism as neither disability nor exceptionalism. It's a fact that Lauren lives with; it shapes her encounters without necessarily limiting them. At the book's core lies a wish that anyone can identify with: the need for a friend. This winsome, gentle introduction to differences will be a positive addition to school and home libraries."—*FOREWORD REVIEWS*

"Lauren's narrative voice is honest, poignant, and spot-on in describing her often baffled perceptions...Bender's pencil-and-digital illustrations appear on nearly every generously leaded spread. Her tender, winsome depictions of Lauren, sometimes endearingly engaged but other times steamy with anger, broaden the tale and make it accessible to even children transitioning to chapter books. This nondidactic effort is a fine, affecting addition to the literature for kids on the spectrum and for those who know those kids—in short, for just about everyone."—*KIRKUS REVIEWS*

"A necessary addition to elementary school libraries and a potential spark for a discussion about autism, Asperger's, or simply embracing differences."—*SCHOOL LIBRARY JOURNAL*

"Bender's pencil drawings readily reflect characters' frustrations and other emotions—feelings that Lauren acknowledges she has trouble recognizing. Leach's empathetic novel should both open eyes and encourage greater patience and understanding."
—*PUBLISHERS WEEKLY*

"Lauren's happier 'butterfly days' become something to root for, as she bonds with her baby sister and eventually makes a friend. Frequent clear pencil and digital illustrations break up the sometimes-long paragraphs and should help young readers understand Lauren's emotions and others' reactions."—*THE HORN BOOK MAGAZINE*

First published in Canada in 2018
First published in the United States in 2019

Text copyright © 2018 Sara Leach
Illustration copyright © 2018 Rebecca Bender
This edition copyright © 2018 Pajama Press Inc.
This is a first edition.

10 9 8 7 6 5 4 3 2 1

www.pajamapress.ca info@pajamapress.ca

 Canada Council   Conseil des arts
for the Arts   du Canada

 ONTARIO ARTS COUNCIL
CONSEIL DES ARTS DE L'ONTARIO
an Ontario government agency
un organisme du gouvernement de l'Ontario

Canadä

The publisher gratefully acknowledges the support of the Canada Council for the Arts and the Ontario Arts Council for its publishing program. We acknowledge the financial support of the Government of Canada through the Canada Book Fund (CBF) for our publishing activities.

Library and Archives Canada Cataloguing in Publication

Leach, Sara, 1971-, author
  Penguin days / by Sara Leach ; illustrations by Rebecca Bender.
ISBN 978-1-77278-053-6 (hardcover)
  I. Bender, Rebecca, illustrator II. Title.
PS8623.E253P46 2018   jC813'.6   C2018-902710-X

Publisher Cataloging-in-Publication Data (U.S.)

Names: Leach, Sara, 1971-, author. | Bender, Rebecca, 1980-, illustrator.
Title: Penguin Days / by Sara Leach; illustrations by Rebecca Bender.
Description: Toronto, Ontario Canada: Pajama Press, 2018. | Summary: "Lauren, who has Autism Spectrum Disorder, reluctantly takes on the role of flower girl in her aunt's wedding. While it's difficult to break her familiar routines and deal with unfamiliar cousins and scratchy dresses, Lauren eventually decides that having an extended family is worth the bother" -- Provided by publisher.
Identifiers: ISBN 978-1-77278-053-6 (hardcover)
Subjects: LCSH: Extended families – Juvenile fiction. | Autism spectrum disorders – Juvenile fiction. | Weddings – Juvenile fiction. | BISAC: JUVENILE FICTION / Social Themes / Special needs. | JUVENILE FICTION / Family / Marriage & Divorce. | JUVENILE FICTION / Social Themes / Emotions & Feelings.
Classification: LCC PZ7.L433Pe |DDC [E] – dc23

Original art created with pencil and digital media
Cover and book design—Rebecca Bender

Manufactured by Friesens
Printed in Canada

Pajama Press Inc.
181 Carlaw Ave. Suite 251 Toronto, Ontario Canada, M4M 2S1

Distributed in Canada by UTP Distribution
5201 Dufferin Street Toronto, Ontario Canada, M3H 5T8

Distributed in the U.S. by Ingram Publisher
1 Ingram Blvd. La Vergne, TN 37086, USA

Chapter 1

IT TOOK US two days, eight movies, four chapter books, and three throw-ups to reach Auntie Joss's house. Mom only flipped her lid twice. Lexi needed twelve diaper changes. Dad kept turning up the sound on the radio and telling us we'd be there soon.

Auntie Joss lived in Lincoln, North Dakota, where it was as flat as our school field. Without all the kids. And with more corn. There were no mountains or oceans, but we did see some tall buildings. Dad said they were grain elevators. I didn't understand why grain would have to go up and down an elevator, but Dad said he didn't know how they worked and was too tired from driving to think about it.

"Lincoln, North Dakota, is a long, long way from home," I said.

"It is," Mom said. "But we're going for a very important reason. Auntie Joss is getting married, and you're going to be a flower girl."

Dad turned down the radio. "It's an extra-special wedding because it will take place in the field behind Auntie Joss's farmhouse."

"You'll walk down the aisle in front of Auntie Joss, and lead her to Charlie," said Mom.

I stuck my hand out the window and let the hot air wave it up and down. "You already told me twice. Auntie Joss should get married at our house. We have flowers in our backyard, not elevators."

Dad turned the radio back up.

At last we arrived at Auntie Joss's house. She came running across the grass and pressed a wet kiss on my cheek.

I said, "Yuck," and wiped it off with my sleeve.

Mom said, "Sorry, Joss, it's been quite a trip." They hugged each other for a long time, while Dad took Lexi out of the car seat and let her walk on the grass. Lexi was just learning to walk and she fell down a lot. I once asked Dad if there was something wrong with her, because she didn't seem to be getting the hang of it. But he said it was normal and I did the same thing when I was her age.

Finally, Mom and Auntie Joss finished hugging. My aunt crouched in front of me and said, "How's my flower girl?"

"I'm fine, thank you. When do I look for the cow poop?"

Auntie Joss tilted her head to the side. "Sorry?"

"When am I going to walk down your farm and spread flowers on the ground so you don't step in cow poop on your way to marry Almost-Uncle Charlie?"

Auntie Joss laughed. "You're precious."

"Gems are precious," I said. "I'm not a gem. But I would like to be an amethyst. They are purple."

Auntie Joss threw her arms in the air and laughed and laughed. Her laughing made me feel jittery. And she still hadn't told me when I would do my flower-girl job. I decided to help Lexi walk.

"The wedding is in two days," Dad said.

I nodded while I held Lexi's hands. Dad knew I liked to have answers to my questions.

"Come see your cousins," Auntie Joss said. "They're in the backyard."

"No thank you," I said. I didn't need any cousins. Lexi was enough family for me. I didn't need more friends either. I already had a best friend named Irma. She rode the bus with me every day. She liked looking for insects on the school grounds, and she liked reading about penguins during partner reading time.

Dad's eyebrow shot up his forehead like a caterpillar on a trampoline. "It's polite to say hi to your cousins, Lauren. You haven't seen them for a very long time."

I hadn't seen my cousins since I was three years old. Dad said the reason we drove to Lincoln, North Dakota, was because the last time we came we flew in an airplane, and nobody wanted to live through the experience of flying with me again.

He said probably all the other passengers on the plane needed to get their hearing checked when they arrived, thanks to all my screaming.

Of course I screamed. I don't like change, and an airplane was not like my house or my school. Mom and Dad always say my brain works differently than other people's brains because I have Autism Spectrum Disorder. They say my different brain is one of the things they love about me. But the other people on the plane didn't know about my brain. So all the screaming made them want to flip their lids. Mom and Dad must have decided it was easier to drive all the way to Lincoln, North Dakota, than to teach the people on the airplane about Autism Spectrum Disorder.

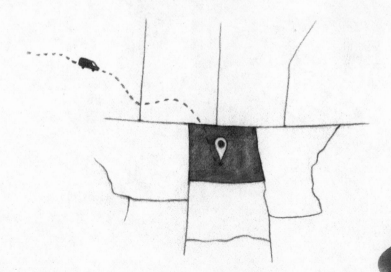

Chapter

2

I FOLLOWED AUNTIE Joss along a concrete stepping path beside the house and into the backyard.

"There's no cow poop here," I said.

"I sure hope not," Auntie Joss said. "The cow plop should stay on the field with the cows."

"Cow plop?"

"That's what we call it in these parts."

I liked the sound of cow plop. *Plop. Plop. Plop.*

"Can we go look for cow plop now?"

"Maybe later," Auntie Joss said. She smiled, which I liked better than her laugh.

I looked for insects as I followed her, since there wasn't any cow plop around. I found three spiders, which have two body parts and eight legs and are definitely not insects.

Two girls and a boy were running around in the backyard. The three kids stopped running in circles and ran toward us instead. "Hi, Lauren!" they shouted. I covered my ears and stepped behind Dad's legs. He moved to the side. I wished he were more like a tree.

The cousins screeched to a stop right in front of me.

I stuck out my hand to the tall girl. "Hi-nice-to-meet-you."

She looked at my hand and giggled. "Don't you remember me?"

I shook my head.

"I'm Sophia." She pointed to the other girl. "That's my sister Zoe. And that's our brother Kevin."

I stuck out my hand again, but they didn't shake it. My special-helper teacher, Ms. Lagorio—whose name meant green lizard but who was a pretty lady—taught me to shake hands and look at people's faces when I met them. I guess my cousins didn't get to have lessons with a special-helper teacher.

The first time we met, my friend Irma shook my hand and said hello. After school finished, she went back to Sweden, but only for the summer. She would be with me for the start of the third grade. We would be in a new class, which was scary, even though I was happy to say goodbye to our old classroom teacher. Mrs. Patel breathed deeply through her nose a lot when she talked to me.

On the last day of school, I gave Mrs. Patel the card I made for her. It said: *Dear Mrs. Patel. Thank you for teaching me this year. My dad says*

he hopes you have a restful summer because you deserve it after teaching me.

Mrs. Patel held the card up in front of her nose, and her eyes got all shiny when she read the card. Usually when people's eyes watered it meant they were sad. I wondered why my card made her sad.

She gave me a hug. "I'm going to miss you, Lauren. I hope you have a restful summer too."

I didn't want to have a restful summer. I wanted to have a fun summer with Irma, looking for insects in the forest. But Irma was in Sweden. Maybe they had forests in Sweden, but they didn't have me there to help her find insects. So I had to meet my cousins instead. Which wasn't restful at all. It made my insides feel like squirmy snakes.

"Put your foot in for tag!" Kevin shouted.

I covered my ears with my hands again. Sophia and Zoe put their feet in next to Kevin's. I stepped behind my dad.

"Don't you want to play?" Sophia asked, peering around his leg.

I shook my head. I wrapped my arms around my dad's waist. I felt cold and hot at the same time. Dad tried to peel my hands off him. I grabbed tighter.

Ms. Lagorio told me that when you felt scared or angry, you were using a very old part of your brain. Older than my dad. Older than the principal. As old as the dinosaurs. She said it was the lizard part of your brain. Whenever I flipped my lid, that was the part I was using. I should try and let the other part of my brain—the thinking part—take control. She taught me some tricks to help, like squeezing my favorite eraser and doing square breathing. But it was still hard to do.

I clung to Dad's waist and tried to get the thinking part of my brain to take control. I did some square breathing. I pictured walking around a square as I breathed. I breathed in and counted to four. Then I turned the corner of the square, held my breath, and counted to four again. I turned again and breathed out for four. Then I held my breath for four on the last side of the square. I remembered to start breathing

again, which was important, because sometimes when I practiced, I forgot and kept holding my breath until Ms. Lagorio tapped me on the shoulder.

Dad nudged me into the backyard and went over to talk to a lady who had been sitting in a chair reading her book. "Hi, Margaret," he said. She put down her book, stood up, and gave him a hug. He hugged her back, so I guessed she was supposed to be there.

Chapter
3

KEVIN STEPPED TOWARD me. "I'm nine. How old are you?"

"Eight," I said.

"I'm ten," Zoe said. She pulled her long, black hair into a ponytail. Then, without saying anything, she did a backflip right in front of me on the grass.

"Show-off!" Kevin said. He ran to a tree, took two steps up the trunk, and jumped high in the air, twisting his body and landing on his feet. "I do parkour."

Sophia said. "I'm twelve. I play soccer. What do you do?"

I stared at Sophia. She was tall and strong. She also had long, black hair.

"I look for insects. And I read."

Sophia scrunched up her nose. "You look for bugs?"

I nodded. "With Irma."

"I like bugs," Kevin said. "What kind do you look for?"

"Whatever I can find." I pointed at the ground. "Like that beetle crawling on the grass." I knelt down and let the black beetle creep onto my hand. It had three body parts and six legs. Its shiny black body was fat, kind of like an army tank.

"Yuck," Sophia said. "I can't believe you picked it up."

"He won't hurt me."

"Can I hold him?" Kevin asked.

I put my hand next to his so the beetle would walk onto his hand. "Be gentle," I said. "Beetles are strong, but you could still hurt him."

Zoe did another back handspring.

"You're like a beetle," I said. "They can flip

their bodies over too. They have a special joint that helps them do it. Do you have a special joint?"

Sophia wrinkled her nose. "No. She just practices a lot."

Auntie Joss came outside. "Time for my flower girls to try on their dresses."

Sophia ran to Auntie Joss. Zoe backflipped over to her.

I stood behind them. "I'm ready."

Auntie Joss gave that funny laugh again. "Excellent. I have my flower girls. My two bridesmaids and the matron of honor are already upstairs trying on their dresses. Let's go get beautiful, girls."

I didn't know why Zoe and Sophia needed to try on a dress since I was the flower girl.

Auntie Joss and the cousins walked inside, but I stayed in the yard with my arms crossed.

"What's wrong?" Kevin asked.

I just shook my head.

"Don't you want to wear a dress? At least you don't have to wear a penguin suit like me."

A penguin suit? Kevin got to wear a *onesie* for the wedding? I definitely wanted to stay out on the grass with him in that case. Unless the brides-maids were wearing onesies too. Maybe Auntie Joss would let me wear a pug onesie. Pugs were my favorite dog. I liked their squashed faces and wrinkles. Even if they did have breathing problems and stuck their tongues out all the time.

I decided to go inside and try on my onesie.

Chapter
4

UPSTAIRS, THERE WEREN'T any onesies around. Instead, three frilly, purple dresses were laid out on the bed. Why would I need three dresses? Actually, I didn't need any dresses, because I would wear a pug onesie.

Sophia picked up one of the dresses. "It's so pretty."

Zoe picked up the other one and crinkled up her face. "It has a lot of frills."

Auntie Margaret said, "Zoe!" in the voice Dad used when I'd said something wrong.

"Well, it's true," Zoe said.

"Don't you like it?" Auntie Joss's voice was a bit trembly.

"Oh, I like it," Zoe said. Her arms were crossed. Ms. Lagorio's cards said that meant she was mad.

Maybe she didn't like the dress. But why didn't she say so?

"It looks scratchy," I said. "I'll wear a pug onesie instead. Please."

Everybody stopped and looked at me.

"Why would you wear a pug onesie?" Sophia asked.

"Kevin is wearing a penguin suit," I said. "So I will wear a pug onesie."

Auntie Joss did her laughing thing again. "Priceless!" she said. "Lauren, you are just priceless."

I stared at her. Of course I was priceless. "Kids don't have prices," I said. Unless she'd been planning on selling me at the end of the wedding. My lizard brain started to take over again. Sparks started going off inside my head.

"Lauren, that's just an expression," Mom said. "Nobody is going to sell you." My thinking brain took over from the lizard. Sometimes it felt like

Mom could see inside my mind.

"Let's try on these dresses," Mom said. She took me into a little bathroom.

The dress felt as itchy as it looked.

"It's beautiful," Mom said. She turned me around so I could see myself in the mirror.

I rubbed my hand under the shoulder strap. I scratched the top of my chest. A pug onesie wouldn't be itchy. It would be soft and cozy. I lifted up the skirt and scratched my legs.

"Oh dear," Mom said. "I think we have a problem."

We went into the bedroom again. Sophia and Zoe were both wearing the same dresses as me. I still didn't know why, since I was the flower girl. We looked like three purple flowers. The kind that grew in my neighbor's garden. I thought being a flower girl meant throwing flowers, not looking like a flower. I reached down the front of my dress and scratched my stomach.

Sophia twirled around so her skirt floated up and down like the swings at the fair. Zoe stood with her arms crossed over her chest. Sophia looked like she was having more fun, so I copied her. I spun as fast as I could and tried looking at my skirt to see if it was spinning. I bonked into Zoe.

"Watch out!" she said.

So I moved away and bonked into Auntie Joss instead.

"Lauren, stop!" Mom said.

I stopped. But the room kept spinning. My stomach didn't feel good.

"You're green!" Mom said.

I looked at my dress. It hadn't turned green.

I threw up. All over the floor. All over Zoe's bare feet. It dribbled down my dress.

"Gross!" Zoe screamed.

"You threw up on her feet!" Sophia yelled.

"Oh dear," Mom said. She grabbed a towel and tried to clean up Zoe's feet.

I stomped downstairs. Zoe and Sophia were mean.

I missed Irma.

Chapter
5

KEVIN WAS STILL in the backyard, practicing
his parkour, which meant running up things and
jumping off them.

"Where are Zoe and Sophia?" he asked.
"What's on your dress?"

"Upstairs." I crossed my arms over my chest so

he would know I was mad, and leaned against the tree because my stomach still felt green.

"What's wrong?"

"They don't like me."

"Wanna see the barn?" he asked.

I thought for a second. I didn't know what was exciting about a big building, but it was farther away from Zoe and Sophia. "Okay."

I followed him through the trees and out into the cornfields behind them. Once we were on the dirt road, there weren't any trees for him to jump off. So he ran instead. I had to run to keep up with him. Which made it hard to look for insects, but meant I moved farther from Zoe and Sophia.

We stopped in front of a giant wooden building with two big doors.

"Follow me," Kevin said. He slid open the door.

I stood with my toes just outside the barn and looked in. It was as big as the swimming pool at the rec center, but it smelled of grass and animal poo instead of chlorine. I couldn't see very far inside because it was dark, but I could hear animals moving around. Big animals.

"Come on," Kevin said. "I need to close the door."

I stayed where I was.

"It's just cows in here. Nothing can hurt you. They're all inside their stalls, anyway."

I took two baby steps inside the barn, and Kevin shut the door behind me. My eyes started getting used to the darkness. There was a big hallway in the middle of the barn. Three cow heads poked through a big open fence on one side.

Kevin ran to one of the cows. "Auntie Joss says we can come in here, but we aren't allowed to touch the cows without an adult around." He leaned his face close to the cow. I guess the cow knew Auntie Joss's rule, because she backed up a step.

"Aren't you going to come see her?" Kevin asked.

I shook my head. I never knew cows were so big.

"C'mon! I thought someone who liked bugs would like cows."

I turned and looked at the wood holding up the barn to search for insects, which were much smaller than cows. But it was too dark to see.

"Listen to this," Kevin said. He cupped his hands over his mouth. "*Moooo*." His voice sounded low and slow.

"*Moooo*," the cow said.

I took a step toward Kevin. "You can speak cow!"

"Yup. My dad taught me." He mooed again.

MOOOOOOO

The cow mooed back.

"What's it saying?"

"She wants to know your name. Come tell her."

"It's a she?" I took a step closer.

"Of course. That's why she's a cow."

I stood near the fence. I put my hands over my mouth. "My naaammme iiiiisss Laurrrennn." I

tried to make my voice low and slow like Kevin's.

The cow didn't say anything back.

"Let me try," said Kevin. He put his hands over his mouth again. "*Moooo.*"

"*Moooo,*" the cow said.

"She says it's nice to meet you. Her name is Henrietta. And she asks if we've met her daughter."

"Her daughter?"

Kevin ran to the other side of the barn. I followed him. Inside one of the other stalls were three little cows. They pushed their noses through the fence at us.

Kevin patted one of them.

"Auntie Joss said not to touch," I said.

"But look at them. Obviously they want us to touch them."

The smallest cow was black and white. I point- ed to it. "Is that one Henrietta's daughter?"

"I'll ask," Kevin said. "*Mooo*?"

The little cows mooed back. But it sounded more like *Maaaa*.

"Yes," Kevin said. "The black-and-white one is Mary Lou, and she belongs to Henrietta."

Mary Lou wasn't nearly as scary as Henriet- ta. She was my height. I put my face close to her. She didn't back away. "Dooo youuu miiiss yourrr mommm?" I asked.

Mary Lou nodded.

I reached toward her. Auntie Joss wouldn't

mind if I patted Mary Lou's head. It would make her miss her mom less. She was soft.

I climbed on the gate to pat her some more. I stroked her back. It wasn't as soft. Mary Lou took a step back so I leaned over the fence a bit more.

I wanted to see if I could touch her tail. I climbed
up higher on the fence. I reached waaay over.

I fell into the stall.

Chapter
6

THE BARN GOT really noisy. Mary Lou
mooed. Kevin yelled. And somebody was screaming. I lay on my back in the prickly hay. Mary Lou
stepped toward me. I curled into a ball, covered
my head with my arms, and started rocking back
and forth.

"Lauren!" Kevin pulled on my arm. "Stop screaming!"

I stopped screaming. The barn got quieter. But I stayed in a ball and rocked back and forth.

"You have to get out of the stall," Kevin said. "Auntie Joss is going to be so mad!"

I didn't care about Auntie Joss. I was too scared of Mary Lou trampling me. I rocked my way further into the corner.

Kevin pushed me and I rolled over onto my back. Now he was in the stall with me. He was standing too close.

"Stop touching me!" I shouted.

"The calves are loose!" Kevin said. "They got out when I came in the stall to help you."

That made me look up. Mary Lou wasn't in the stall anymore. Neither were the other baby cows. I was safe. Except the baby cows were running around the barn. And the mama cows were mooing like crazy.

"The mamas want their babies," I said. "Should we let the mamas out too?"

"No!" Kevin shouted. "We're in enough trouble. Help me get them back in."

The barn door slid open. I stood up to see who was there. All I could see was the outline of a very tall, skinny man. I curled up in my ball again.

"Uncle Charlie!" Kevin shouted. "Close the door! Lauren let the calves out of their stall!"

I stood up. "I did not let them out! I fell in and they almost trampled me!"

The man, who must have been my Almost-Uncle Charlie, shut the barn door behind him. "What happened?"

I opened my mouth to tell him, but he held up a hand, which meant Stop.

"Never mind. You can tell me later. We need to get these calves back in the stall."

"But they want to be with their mamas," I said.

Kevin elbowed me in the ribs. I elbowed him back.

"Lauren!" he shouted.

"Kevin!" I stomped on his foot. It felt good.

A hand grabbed my arm. Another hand grabbed Kevin's arm.

"Quit it, you two. I need help." Almost-Uncle Charlie leaned down and looked in my eyes. "I don't know what happened, but I do know what's going to happen. You two are going to stop fighting and help me wrangle these calves back where they belong. Kevin, bring me a rope from that wall. Lauren, stand by the door to the stall and get ready to close it when I get them inside."

I stood behind the stall door and did my square breathing while Almost-Uncle Charlie herded the calves into the stall. As soon as

they were all in, Kevin helped me push the door closed.

Almost-Uncle Charlie looked down at us. I tilted my head to look way up at him.

"Lauren," he said. His voice was low. My insides were squirmy.

He smiled, knelt down, and held out his hand. "It's nice to meet you. I've heard a lot about you."

I shook his hand and remembered to look in his eyes. I liked Almost-Uncle Charlie. He could wrangle cows and he knew his manners.

I liked him even more when he told me his family came from Sweden.

"Do you know Irma?" I asked. "She's my best friend."

Almost-Uncle Charlie rubbed his hand against his chin. "I don't think I know any Irmas. But if I meet one I'll be sure to ask her if she knows you."

"If she likes to look at insects and read books, then she's my Irma."

Almost-Uncle Charlie put a hand to his chin again and nodded. "I'll remember that." He stood up so Kevin and I had to tilt our heads up to see him again. "Listen, you two. The next time you want to look at the cows, you need to bring an adult. We don't want any animals on the loose with the wedding happening tomorrow."

"Okay, Uncle Charlie," Kevin said. "We won't."

I nodded. The last thing we needed was more cow plop in the aisle. That would be a disaster.

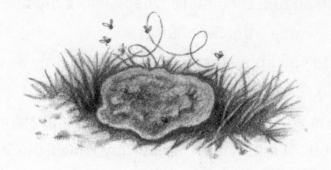

Chapter 7

THAT AFTERNOON MOM took me shopping at the mall. After the throw-up and rolling on the barn floor, my dress didn't look so good. Mom said I couldn't buy a pug onesie, or a penguin suit either. But we did buy a nice, soft, purple dress.

"It's too bad you won't match the other flower girls," Mom said. "At least you won't be scratching all the way down the aisle."

"Why do I have to match? I'm the only flower girl."

Mom stopped and looked at me. "No, honey. Zoe and Sophia are flower girls too. That's why they have purple dresses. Didn't we tell you that?"

I shook my head.

"You had fun twirling with Sophia today, didn't you?"

"Until I threw up. She called me gross."

"Don't you think it will be fun to be part of a group of flower girls?"

I shook my head. The volcano started to simmer inside me. I didn't like it when things changed. And I didn't like sharing.

Mom's face froze like an ice cube. I tried to think of the cards Ms. Lagorio showed me with people's faces on them. It definitely wasn't a happy look. Or sad. Or even angry. She looked around the store. I wondered if there was someone she was hoping to see.

"Lauren," Mom said, "I don't have your eraser. And I can see you are about to flip your lid. But this really isn't a good place to do it." She took a deep breath. "Why don't you breathe with me?"

I shook my head. The volcano bubbled some more.

Her face moved again like the ice melted because she'd had a very smart idea. "You know," she said, "I'm the matron of honor. Which is like a special bridesmaid. I bet Auntie Joss would be okay if you were the flower girl of honor."

I tilted my head and thought. "Is there only one of those?"

Mom nodded. "And she gets to wear a different dress than everyone else."

I looked down at my nice soft purple dress. "Okay."

Mom let out her big breath and we went to pay.

When we returned to Auntie Joss's I went into the TV room and Mom rushed over and started whispering with Auntie Joss. Auntie Joss did her laughing thing again. I put my hands over my ears and tried to ignore her. They called Zoe and Sophia over and whispered some more. Zoe and Sophia both frowned. "Why does she get to be special?" Zoe asked. Mom whispered some more. Zoe and Sophia shrugged and said, "Okay." They went back to their TV watching.

I pulled my dress out of the shopping bag. I rubbed my hand across the soft fabric. It was the next best thing to a pug onesie. It might even be better than a penguin suit.

Chapter

8

A MAN WITH black hair walked into the room carrying Lexi. "Anybody lose a baby?" he asked.

I jumped off the couch. "That's my baby!" I ran to take Lexi from him.

He opened his mouth wide and showed me a

bunch of white teeth. "Hi, Lauren. Remember me?"

I stepped closer and looked at his face. He had dark, shiny hair like my cousins, but his face was browner and more wrinkly. I didn't know him, but his face looked like Ms. Lagorio's "friendly" card, so I wasn't scared of him. "No, I don't know you." I held my hands out for Lexi.

"I'm your Uncle Raymond!"

"Hi, Dad," Kevin said.

"Oh," I said. It's nice to meet you." I couldn't shake his hand because of Lexi. She gurgled at me and tried to grab my hair. I put her on the ground. "Show Uncle Raymond how you can walk." Lexi wobbled back and forth a few times, took three steps toward Kevin, then dropped onto her bum. It was a good thing she had the diaper on for padding.

I held out my two pointer fingers for Lexi to grab onto and helped her stand. She waddled toward Uncle Raymond. I waddled behind her.

"*Quack, quack,*" I said.

Uncle Raymond clapped his hands and laughed. I liked Uncle Raymond. He laughed when I was funny.

"Kevin says you can speak cow," I said.

Uncle Raymond nodded. "I hear you spent some time in the barn today."

"Yes. I'm not going back there. Can you moo for Lexi?"

Uncle Raymond put both hands over his mouth. "*Moooooooooooo,*" he said. It sounded just like there was a cow in the TV room. I wondered if Mary Lou heard him.

Lexi fell again. She started to cry. I picked her up and squeezed her. "Don't be scared. He's just speaking cow. It's another language. Like French. I can speak duck. *Quack, quack!*"

Lexi laughed, so I did it some more. "*Quack, quack, quack, quack.*"

"That's enough, Lauren," Mom said.

"*Mooooooooooo,*" Uncle Raymond said.

"Dad!" Sophia said.

"*Moooooooo?*" Uncle Raymond asked.

Sophia didn't speak cow. Uncle Raymond, Lexi, and I walked outside so we could practice our walking and our languages in peace.

Chapter 9

THE NEXT AFTERNOON, it was time for the wedding rehearsal. I put on my soft, purple dress, but Mom said we had to make sure it stayed clean because there wasn't time for us to go shopping again. I wore my soft leggings instead. Auntie Joss didn't wear her wedding dress either. She wore a nice white dress that looked very comfortable. I would have liked to get married in a dress like that. If I were getting married. Which I was never going to do, because getting married meant liking a boy. Like Dan. Which I *didn't*.

"Calling all ring bearers and flower girls," Dad said.

Sophie, Zoe, and Kevin ran to Dad, who was standing at the back door.

"Lauren?" Dad said. "Why aren't you coming?"

"You didn't say flower girl of honor. That's me."

Dad rubbed his forehead. "Right. Calling all flower girls of honor."

I joined the cousins at the door.

Dad led us to the field next to the backyard. Instead of rows of corn, there were rows of chairs.

A white arch covered in sunflowers stood at the front of the rows.

"This is where the wedding will be," Dad said. "Today we're going to practice."

The aunties and Mom were already there. So were Uncle Raymond and Almost-Uncle Charlie. They were talking to a lady I didn't know.

"This is Fran," Almost-Uncle Charlie said. "She's our marriage commissioner. That means she's going to lead the ceremony tomorrow."

Fran crouched and smiled at us all. "Are you guys ready to rock-and-roll?"

Zoe and Sophia nodded. Kevin played an air guitar and jumped around. I stared at Fran. We were practicing a wedding, not a rock concert.

Fran stood. "Do we have everybody?"

Auntie Joss nodded. "Yup. Let's get this party started."

I looked at Dad. "I thought the party was tomorrow."

"Figure of speech," he said. "I'll explain later."

Mom handed Zoe, Sophia, and me each an empty woven basket.

"You'll have to pretend there are flower petals in your baskets, girls. We aren't going to pick the real flowers until tomorrow morning."

Auntie Margaret showed us how to walk down the aisle between the chairs. We had to reach into our empty baskets and pretend to pull out handfuls of flower petals and scatter them on the ground. I couldn't see any cow plop in the aisle, but maybe we were pretending about that part too.

"Right," said Fran. "Why don't we give it a try? I gather we have a flower girl of honor?"

I stepped forward so my toes were almost touching Fran's. "That's me."

Fran nodded and took a step back. "Excellent. You can go first, followed by the two flower girls. Then our bridesmaids, and finally the bride. Ring bearer and groom, you start at the front with me."

I started down the aisle. Pretending to throw flowers on the ground was boring, so I decided to throw them in the air instead. I imagined I was throwing a rainbow of flowers from my hand and they were floating through the air and scattering on the ground.

"Lauren," my mom called from her spot at the back of the aisle, "You need to keep walking. Your job is to walk down the aisle and scatter flowers, not do an interpretive dance."

I ran the rest of the way to the arch.

"Why don't we try that again," Fran said.

I had to walk all the way to the back of the aisle.

"Right," said Fran. "Remember to walk slowly."

I inched forward, pretending I was a sloth. I walked very, very slowly, and threw my flowers very, very slowly. Sloths move slowly to conserve energy. And they can turn their heads in almost a full circle. I tried moving my head all the way around in a circle, but I didn't get very far. All I saw was Mom, Zoe, and Sophia shooing me forward.

"Lauren, maybe you could walk a little faster," Fran said.

I sighed. I wished these people would make up their minds. I walked quickly to the arch where Fran was standing. Zoe and Sophia came down the aisle after me.

Fran smiled. "I think we'll call that good enough. Bridesmaids, you can start."

The rest of the rehearsal was boring. Fran let Sophia, Zoe, and me sit in the chairs while the adults walked up and down the aisle and talked. Kevin stepped forward with a tiny pillow, which would have made a good bed for a beetle, and handed it to Almost-Uncle Charlie. For some reason that made everybody get shiny eyes.

Chapter 10

AFTER THE REHEARSAL ended, we all went to the restaurant together. I ate my plain noodles with butter and walked over to where Mom was sitting.

"Time to go," I said.

"Lauren, the adults haven't even been served

yet. Go talk to your cousins."

I went back to the kids' table. The cousins were still eating their pasta with red sauce. I told them facts about penguins, which was more interesting than sitting around waiting for the adults.

"Penguins can drink saltwater. And they sneeze it out. Rockhopper penguins have spiky yellow hair. Like Almost-Uncle Charlie. Emperor penguins feed their babies by regurgitating their food into their mouths. Regurgitating means throwing up."

"That's gross, Lauren," Zoe said. She dropped her fork onto her noodles and pushed the plate to the middle of the table.

"I don't wanna hear anything more about penguins," Kevin said.

I started to tell him about lizards instead. "Lizards smell with their tongues. There is one kind

of lizard that squirts blood from its eyes to pro-
tect itself."

"I have to go to the bathroom," Kevin said, and
pushed his chair back.

"Me too," said Sophia.

"Me three," said Zoe.

I didn't have to pee, so I waited at the table.
But they were slow like sloths so I went to see
what they were doing.

They weren't even going to the bathroom! There
was a chalkboard in the hallway and they were
drawing on it. Zoe was drawing a green unicorn.
Sophia had drawn a city and was adding flying cars.
Kevin was drawing a gigantic robot with antennae
sticking out of its head.

Chalk felt squeaky on my fingers, so I didn't
want to do any drawing. Instead, I told Kevin
more facts about lizards. "Some lizards can lose
their tail to avoid predators. It will grow back, but

without any bone."

Kevin erased the robot's mouth and eyebrows. He drew a zigzag line for the mouth, and made the eyebrows slant like slides. His robot looked like the angry face Ms. Lagorio showed me.

"Why is your robot mad?" I asked.

"He doesn't like lizards," Kevin said. Sophia started giggling. Zoe laughed so hard she dropped her chalk.

I stopped telling him facts and turned away from the angry robot. Kevin might be nicer than Sophia and Zoe, but he could still be mean.

Chapter

11

DAD WOKE ME up the next morning. "Are you
ready for your big day?" His face looked like he was
excited. I wondered if there was a big surprise.

"Are we going to the ice-cream store?" I asked.

He laughed. "No. Auntie Joss and Uncle Charlie
are getting married today!"

"Oh," I said. "I'll stay in bed." I didn't want Dad to be disappointed, so I added, "Thank you," to be polite.

Dad pulled the covers off of me and made his buzzer sound. "Nice try. Everyone is counting on our flower girl of honor."

I sat up in bed so he would leave. I wasn't going to the wedding. My cousins weren't anything like Irma. They didn't want to talk about penguins or lizards or beetles. They thought I was gross.

I wished Irma weren't so far away.

I wished weddings had never been invented.

Dad came back in. "Up and at 'em!" he said.

I sighed and rolled out of bed. At least I would get to wear my soft purple dress.

Chapter
12

ZOE AND SOPHIA were excited because they were going to wear makeup to the wedding. Nobody told me about makeup. I stood beside Kevin.

"Are you wearing makeup?" I asked.

"No way!" he said.

"Then me neither."

Kevin was wearing a pair of black pants, a white shirt, and a black jacket. He had a funny tie with two triangles around his neck. He kept pulling at the tie.

"Where's your penguin onesie?" I asked.

He tilted his head. "Huh?"

"You said you get to wear a penguin suit to the wedding."

Kevin shook his head. "Don't you know anything?" He pointed to his outfit. "Black and white? I look like a penguin. Get it?"

I looked at his feet to see if they were webbed, and lifted up his arm to check for flippers.

"Stop!"

I dropped his arm. "You don't look like a penguin." Maybe he should have asked for the makeup after all. It might have helped with the costume.

"Time to go," Uncle Raymond said.

We lined up at the door and Uncle Raymond led us across the backyard and into the field. He told us to wait under the trees so the guests couldn't see us. I peeked around the tree. The field looked like it had the day before, with the archway and the aisle. But instead of rows of empty chairs, there were rows of chairs full of people.

People I would have to walk past.

People who would be looking at me.

People I didn't know.

Uncle Raymond came back with Dad, Lexi, Kevin, Mom, Auntie Margaret, and Auntie Joss. "Everybody ready?" he asked.

I didn't answer. My lizard brain was too busy setting off fireworks inside my head.

Chapter 13

KEVIN PEERED AT me. "Are you okay?"

I stared at him.

"You look kinda green," he said. "You aren't going to throw up again, are you?"

If I kept my mouth closed I wouldn't throw up.

Auntie Joss said, "The guests are all here. It's

time for the flower girls to get started."

I stared at her. My eyes were the only part of my body that could move. Except my brain, which was going a million miles an hour and telling me how many people were sitting in those chairs.

My mom came over. "Time to do your flower-girl-of-honor job, Lauren."

The fireworks went off even louder.

My dad stood in front of me with Lexi. "Lauren, get moving. Everyone is waiting for you."

My lizard brain just kept spinning faster and faster. It was like the lizard was zapping hundreds of flies. *It's too scary. Zap! Don't move. Zap! They'll laugh at you. Zap! You'll do it wrong. Zap!*

Uncle Raymond crouched beside me. "*Moooooooo? Quack quack?*" But the lizard brain had made me forget how to speak cow and duck. Uncle Raymond stood up and waved Sophia, Zoe, and Kevin over. "You guys talk to her," he said.

"What are we supposed to say?" Kevin asked.

Uncle Raymond pulled the cousins into a group a few steps away from me. They bent their heads together. I only heard the words *different* and *friend*.

My lizard brain started going even crazier. Were they going to make fun of me again?

They all walked back toward me. Sophia whispered in my ear. "Auntie Joss needs your help. She needs your flowers to show her the way down the aisle."

I looked at her. Really? Auntie Joss couldn't figure that out? Poor Almost-Uncle Charlie.

Zoe whispered in my other ear. "You make the best rainbow shapes with your flowers."

Kevin stood right in front of me. "This year I had to give a speech in front of the whole school. I was so scared. But my mom told me to imagine everyone was in their underwear, and that made it easier."

I scrunched up my face. I didn't want to imagine anyone in their underwear.

"Kevin, that's gross!" Sophia said. "That'll never work."

"Then imagine they're penguins," he said.

A few penguins waddled in to watch the fireworks going off in my brain.

Sophia passed me a rock. "Mom says you like to squeeze things. Try this."

I took the rock and squeezed it as hard as I could. The fireworks got a bit smaller.

"Do you think you could try?" Zoe said, handing me the basket of flower petals.

My thinking brain took over from the lizard. I nodded.

"Thank goodness," Auntie Joss whispered.

I held my basket of flowers and stepped into the field.

Everybody turned to look at me. My lizard brain almost took over again, but I turned those faces into penguins. I imagined spiky yellow hair on some and webbed feet and black and orange beaks on the others.

I walked slowly down the aisle—but not as slowly as a sloth. I tossed rainbow arcs of flower petals to the Rockhoppers on the left and the Emperors on the right. When I arrived at the arch, I stopped and waited for my cousins to join me. When Auntie Joss reached Almost-Uncle Charlie, we sat on the bench at the front.

The rest of the wedding was boring. I slid off the bench and searched for insects. When Real-Uncle Charlie and Auntie Joss kissed it was gross, but the adults clapped and cheered. Then Auntie Joss and Real-Uncle Charlie walked down the aisle together. Real-Uncle Charlie gave me a thumbs-up as he passed.

Everybody else stood up and made a big crowd at the end of the aisle.

There were so many people. They were too loud. The fireworks started to spark again.

"Let's play on the tractor," Kevin said. He pointed in the opposite direction of all the people. "Nobody's over there. And there's a big grassy field on the other side."

I looked at my three cousins. The fireworks fizzled out. Maybe I could use more relatives than just Lexi.

I nodded at him. "When we get there, let's play tag."

Because playing tag is something friends do.

Author's Note

Lauren lives with ASD or Autism Spectrum Disorder, which means her brain works differently than other people's brains. Among other differences, she has trouble understanding jokes and reading people's facial expressions. But Lauren, like the millions of children around the world with ASD, also experiences feelings to which we can all relate. As I wrote *Penguin Days*, I thought a lot about myself as a child. I never liked it when adults laughed and I didn't get the joke, it hurt not to be included, and I would always have chosen a pug onesie over a scratchy dress.

Rainbow flower-baskets of gratitude to Gail Winskill, Ann Featherstone, and the rest of the team at Pajama Press for allowing me to continue telling Lauren's story. A barnful of thanks to Rebecca Bender for your beautiful illustrations that capture Lauren perfectly. A Rockhopper colony of appreciation to Katherine Fawcett, Stella Harvey, Mary Macdonald, Libby McKeever, Sue Oakey-Baker, and Rebecca Wood Barrett for your suggestions that made Ann's job so much easier. Mooooooch thanks to Annie, for being my eagle-eyed first reader. And I've saved three soft pug onesies for my loving support crew, Duane, Ben, and Julia.